Part I
The Fall of a Giant

Chapter 1
Scandal

Carl stood on the balcony of his office at the top of a skyscraper in the heart of Los Angeles. He gazed out at the city, which seemed to pulse with energy, as though it fed on his success. He was in his world, where every gesture and decision were like moves of pawns on a chessboard—precise and sure. In the film industry, he was more than just a producer. He was a king, capable with a single signature of either lighting up someone's life or destroying it. Every premiere, every film project that came under his wing, became a hit, and his influence grew with every award and contract.

His employees feared him, but respected him. His colleagues spoke of him with admiration, though behind his back, they whispered about his ruthlessness. Few knew his true nature. It revealed itself in closed meetings in private offices, where boundaries were pushed, and deals were struck at a price that no one would publicly accept. His charisma was undeniable, and his words had the power to exert pressure and manipulation that few could resist.

However, clouds began to gather over his empire. The first rumors emerged among the whispers of his staff, then in small articles that lacked the force to break through to the front pages. Carl ignored them with his typical cold smile. "This is not the first time someone's tried to destroy me," he would repeat, burying himself in work, meetings, and events that consumed his life.

Everything changed one evening during the gala premiere of his latest film. In the midst of the banquet, his phone began vibrating incessantly. The messages flooding in were like a warning of an impending storm. Major news outlets began publishing testimonies from women who spoke of his behavior—not only as a man of ambition but as someone who had used his position for things he had never been publicly accused of before.

A media storm began. Behind-the-scenes talks turned into official statements. Famous faces, who once smiled beside him on the red carpet, now either remained silent or issued statements of solidarity with the victims. The pressure mounted until the summons to court arrived. Carl knew that the life he had known was over. Each day of the trial brought to light stories he had tried to bury deep in the past.

In the courtroom, his face, once so confident, was now cold and stiff. The cameras, which once followed him like a shadow, were now witnesses to his downfall. The media scrutinized every detail, and photographs from the trial spread rapidly around the world. Public condemnation was swift and merciless.

At the end of the first day, when the court adjourned, Carl stood before a crowd of reporters and remained silent. This time, he had no words to conceal the truth, nor manipulations that could alter his fate. He understood that his empire, which he had built over decades, was beginning to crumble.

Chapter 2

The Trial and Verdict

The courtroom was filled with people. It echoed with voices and whispers. Carl, sitting on the defendant's bench, felt the weight of hundreds of gazes upon him. Each one was like a needle, piercing him through. Once, the world had admired his elegance, charm, and unquestionable authority. Now, every face staring at him from the gallery reminded him of the fall he had never expected.

The trial was a spectacle whose direction he could no longer control. The first weeks were spent questioning witnesses—both women and men who had been silent observers of his actions for years. Each of their testimonies struck him like shards of glass, reminding him of every moment when he had chosen power over humanity. For many years, Carl had believed he was untouchable, that his influence and money were enough to hide the darkest secrets. But now he was face to face with the brutal truth: no fortune could silence the echoes of guilt and justice.

The first witness was a woman named Sarah. She stood, holding the edge of the podium with trembling hands. She was young, with a voice so soft that the judge had to ask her to speak louder. Her account wasn't particularly dramatic, but it sounded truthful, as if she had finally been able to free herself from a burden she had carried for years. She spoke of an evening when she was called to Carl's office for a new role. She knew something was wrong, but ambition urged her to go. What happened next was vague in her story, but it was enough to draw murmurs of disbelief from the room.

Carl sat, trying to maintain a mask of indifference. But each minute grew harder. When the judge called for another break, Carl felt his heart quicken. Around him, people swarmed—his lawyers, still trying to come up with some defense strategy, journalists eagerly collecting every new piece of information, and the audience who couldn't tear their eyes away from the unfolding drama. They all seemed to be waiting for his reaction, any sign of emotion. But he remained silent, knowing that any word he spoke would only make things worse.

The following weeks were even more difficult. More witnesses presented their stories, and the media buzzed with commentary and analysis. Soon, Carl's trial became a symbol of the fight against violence and abuse, and in society, calls for more decisive actions began to grow. Politicians and activists started a debate on introducing new regulations to ensure the safety of sexual assault victims and to punish perpetrators in ways that would have lasting consequences.

Finally, after three months of relentless bombardment with evidence, it was time for the final word. Carl stood, his hands—once so confident in their gestures—now trembling. The courtroom fell silent. He took a deep breath and looked into the judge's eyes. "I admit that there were moments I now regret," he began. His voice sounded dry, as if it were coming from a throat that had long since stopped speaking sincere words. "I can't turn back time or change what happened. What is happening to me now is part of a process I must accept."

The judge, unmoved by his words, delivered the verdict. "You are found guilty on all charges. In light of the new law, I sentence you to chemical castration and five years under supervision in a specialized therapeutic center." The silence that followed was terrifying. Carl felt his heart race, and his thoughts swirled. The verdict was harsh, but not only in terms of punishment. It was a symbol of the transformations that were yet to come.

The media immediately spread photographs and recordings. Comments flooded in every possible form—from condemnation to words of support for the victims. Debates on television programs, voices from the streets, articles, and op-eds analyzed the significance of the new law, and Carl became not only a criminal but also a symbol of the fall of the old order.

The transfer to the therapeutic center was another blow. There, among men who shared his fate, he began to understand that the sentence was not only the loss of his physical abilities. It was a transformation that forced him to confront himself, his past, and who he had been for all those years.

Daily therapy sessions, meetings with psychologists, and conversations with other convicts were things he had never expected. Where there had once been pride and arrogance, silence and reflection began to emerge.

Chapter 3

Forced Change

The first days after the procedure felt like a dream from which Carl couldn't wake up. The hospital walls, cold and sterile, seemed to press in on him, trapping him in a cage he didn't understand and couldn't escape. The word "punishment" had once seemed abstract to him, something that happened to others. Now he could taste it—bitter, leaving a residue that choked every breath he took.

Carl couldn't find a shred of peace within himself. Since the verdict had been passed and he underwent the procedure of chemical castration, his life had become a series of unfamiliar emotions that disrupted what he had once considered his unshakable nature. He was angry at himself, at society, at everything that had led him to this point. Rage filled his body, but it had nowhere to go. What once fueled his determination now only bred frustration, which he couldn't escape.

Every morning, Carl woke up, staring at the ceiling. His eyes wandered across the white patches of paint, and his thoughts immediately returned to the days gone by. Everything he had, every success, every person he had used for his own gain, now seemed like a shadow of reality. His body was the testament to a new reality—without power, without the strength he had once considered his greatest weapon.

The days in the therapeutic center followed a routine, one that had its highs and lows. The staff consisted of people who knew how to deal with cases like his. In the first days after the procedure, Carl avoided making eye contact with anyone. The sense of shame burned him like a hot iron rod, and every step through the corridor full of other patients was a trial in confronting the new "self" that hadn't yet figured out how to find its place.

Therapy sessions were mandatory. In the dark room, where the light was dimmed by curtains, the therapist, a man with gentle eyes and graying temples, looked at Carl with empathy that he didn't want to accept. "You need to understand that the process of healing begins with acceptance," he said quietly, as if trying to convince not only Carl, but also himself.

Carl clenched his hands on his knees, hearing these words. What could he accept? Who was he supposed to become? Every conversation with the therapist reminded him that now his life was being governed by new rules, rules he hadn't set. He had once been a master of manipulation, and now he had to submit to the rules that confined him and forced him to reflect. Over time, he began to notice something stirring within him—something that had never had the chance to surface before. At first, it was just a small spark of awareness that he had to look at himself from a distance.

The first weeks passed slowly, and Carl found that his thoughts drifted toward the past. He remembered faces—people he had abandoned, people he had hurt. Images of women who had once been nothing more than puppets in his game for success began to haunt him in his dreams. He dreamt of rooms he had once filled with laughter, but in his dreams, the laughter sounded artificial, as though he couldn't recognize it anymore.

His body slowly adapted to the new situation. The changes that had come after the procedure were not only physical but also psychological. His former drive for competition and conquest had vanished, replaced by a strange apathy. But in this apathy, he began to notice elements that had never mattered to him before. He observed the other patients who shared his fate, but they reacted to him differently. Some sought contact, while others avoided it with a similar fear.

One day, as he sat on a bench in the center's courtyard, an older man with a weary face and expressive eyes approached him. "I went through this ten years ago," he began, sitting beside Carl without invitation. His voice was raspy, and his hands trembled slightly as he reached for a cigarette. "It doesn't change a person the way you think it will. But it gives you time to think about who you are without the things that were taken from you."

Carl looked at him, then turned his gaze away, staring into the distance. He thought about what the man had said, and felt that something in his heart, the smallest fragment, was beginning to stir.

Chapter 4

A New Perspective

The first months after the procedure blended together for Carl into a uniform mass of memories. His days were similar to each other—monotonous and silent, filled with therapy sessions and long, solitary walks around the grounds of the center. But something was starting to change, almost imperceptibly. It was like a breeze that touches the skin, though its source is never visible.

One morning, as he sat at a table in the cafeteria, sipping bitter coffee, he noticed something that had previously escaped his attention. A pair of nurses, talking softly in the corner, exchanged smiles that were genuine and warm. He watched them, and for the first time in years, he didn't see them as mere tools for manipulation or people who could serve his interests. They were simply human, and their lives and emotions seemed to exist independently of him.

This discovery struck him like a wave. Carl, who had once seen the world through the lens of his power, now had to face the reality that his role had changed. He was no longer the center of the universe. He had become one of many—one of those who simply existed, without any advantage over others. Throughout his life, his relationships had been transactions; every smile, every gesture, every word had a purpose and was calculated with cold precision. Now, he looked at the people around him with a new, unfamiliar feeling.

In the following weeks, Carl began to notice that the absence of sexual drive affected how he perceived people. He often sat in the common room, observing the conversations of other patients, and saw how their relationships were not underpinned by competition or a desire for dominance. He watched one of the patients, a young man with an uncertain gaze, talking to a woman who worked at the center. They talked about music, laughed at small jokes, and for the first time, Carl saw that simple things could have value in themselves.

He was beginning to realize that his world had once been black-and-white, but now shades of gray were starting to appear. The reflection that overcame him wasn't easy. Every thought about how he had treated people, how he had exploited their weaknesses, brought up a feeling that resembled a burning shame. With each passing reflection, he understood that his methods, which he had once considered effective and indisputable, were not only outdated but deeply harmful. Manipulating, intimidating, exploiting—all of this had been part of his old life, which now seemed as distant as the memory of youthful dreams.

During one of the therapy sessions, the therapist asked Carl how he saw himself now. He sat in silence for a long moment, then looked at her with an expression that, for the first time in a long while, wasn't a mask. "I don't know," he finally replied, his voice sounding foreign even to him. The therapist smiled slightly, as if she had been waiting for exactly that. "That's a good start," she said, writing something in her notebook.

More and more, memories of moments he had once dismissed as insignificant came back to him. He remembered meeting a young actress who had come to him, hoping for a leading role. He had been in his office then, surrounded by luxury, which he had taken for granted as part of his life. She had come, full of passion and dreams, and he had treated her like a pawn, deciding whether she had value to him. Now, looking back on that moment from a new perspective, he felt a bitterness that wouldn't fade. He understood that for her, that meeting could have been a pivotal moment, while for him, it had been just another day, another transaction.

But the process of transformation was not simple. The anger he had felt at the beginning still surfaced in moments of weakness. Often, he would go to sleep with a sense of helplessness that ate at him from the inside. How long would it take before he truly accepted who he had become? Would he ever be able to look at himself without disgust?

Chapter 5

Work anew

Returning to work was like stepping into a world Carl knew, but no longer understood. Just a few years earlier, his presence on a film set had commanded respect, and every order he gave was followed without hesitation. Now, as he crossed the threshold of the production studio, he felt the eyes glide over him with distance. In some, there was disbelief, while in others—clear reservation. Even those who had previously tried to remain indifferent to his downfall now avoided his gaze.

The first days were difficult. Carl took a modest office at the end of the hall, far from the command center that had once been his kingdom. The interior was sparse, with a simple desk, a chair, and a few folders stacked on the shelves. Instead of portraits of Golden Globe winners and posters of his most profitable films, the walls were bare. There were no traces of his former power—only silence and isolation, which echoed through the room.

Carl knew he had to act. It wasn't enough to just return—he had to prove that he had changed, that the new person he was becoming had something valuable to offer. After long, sleepless nights where his thoughts circled around how to regain the industry's respect and his own sense of worth, he came up with an idea that could shift public perception—a film based on the real stories of women who had experienced abuse.

The project wasn't going to be easy. He knew that every move he made would be observed, judged, and criticized. But it was his way of showing remorse, of giving a voice to those who had been ignored for years—those who had become victims of a system he had been part of.

For the first few weeks, Carl faced resistance. When he presented his idea at a team meeting, the reactions were mixed. Some looked at him with suspicion, others with open skepticism. "Why should we believe this is authentic?" asked one of the younger producers, who had always seen him as a relic of the past. Her voice was firm, her eyes cold.

Carl paused for a moment, taking a deep breath. "I don't expect you to trust me right away," he replied, looking her straight in the eyes.

"But I believe we need to do this, not for me, but for those who never had the chance to tell their stories." These words hung in the air, and the room fell silent. There was something in his tone that sounded different than ever before—gone was the arrogance, replaced by humility.

Over time, Carl began working on the screenplay. For the first time in years, he wasn't focused on calculations, on thinking about what award he could win or how the film would be received at Cannes or Berlin. What mattered was the truth. He met with women who wanted to share their stories. Each meeting was a lesson he accepted with respect. He listened to their words, felt their pain, and was ashamed of what he had once represented.

One of the women, who shared her story, left a particularly lasting impression on him. Her name was Marta, and she had once been an aspiring actress. Her career had ended before it even really began, and she had avoided the film industry for years, living far away from the spotlight. When she spoke, her voice trembled, but her gaze was full of determination. "This isn't easy," she said, looking at Carl. "But if my experience can help someone else, I want to do it."

The work on the film began to attract media attention. At first, the reactions were extreme—from praise for his courage and attempt at redemption, to accusations of a cynical bid to regain favor. Carl knew this would happen. Every interview, every public appearance, was a test of his new identity. He responded calmly, avoiding old habits that would have him manipulate his words. Instead, he spoke about the women, their strength, and his new role as a listener, not a dictator.

The hardest moment came on the day the team began the first rehearsal sessions. He was there, on set, but this time as someone who watched from the sidelines, not dictating the terms. He observed as the actresses performed scenes that reflected the stories he had heard. In their eyes, he saw something he had never noticed before— genuine emotion, not directed by him, but born from the depth of their experiences.

As time passed, the team began responding to Carl with less reservation. Seeing his dedication and how he approached the work with newfound humility, they started to realize that his transformation wasn't just superficial. One of the cameramen, who had known Carl for years, came up to him one day after filming had finished. "I don't know if I'll ever fully trust you," he said, looking at him closely. "But I see that you're trying. And that means something."

The film was becoming not just an artistic project but a personal one. Carl knew this was his chance to change—not just in the industry, but within himself.

Chapter 6

Cooperation and trust

As the film project began to take shape, Carl knew that its success would depend on the people involved. Every detail, every scene had to be perfected to touch the viewer and convey the true stories and emotions. On the horizon appeared Anna, a young actress whose passion and talent were gaining increasing recognition. Her casting in the lead role was obvious—she was someone who could breathe life into the characters representing the voice of the victims.

Anna had a reputation as someone unafraid to speak the truth and unwilling to settle for half-measures. When Carl first offered her the role, they met in a small café on the corner behind the film studio. The atmosphere was tense. Carl noticed that Anna had arrived early and taken a seat by the window, watching him with concealed skepticism. Her deep, sharp eyes revealed more than any words she spoke.

"Thank you for coming," Carl began, trying to sound calm, though there was a note of tension in his voice. Anna looked at him without smiling, nodding slightly. She was attentive, as though analyzing every word he said, every change in his expression.

"I know you have many doubts," he added after a moment of silence. "And you're right to have them."

"Tell me one thing," she responded after a longer pause. Her voice was measured, but not friendly. "Why me? Why should I be the face of your redemption?"

The question, though sharp, was valid. Carl took a deep breath, trying to collect his thoughts. He knew he couldn't afford to use empty words or any attempt at manipulation. He had to be honest—even if it meant exposing his weaknesses.

"I'm not looking for redemption," he finally replied, his voice growing more confident. "I'm looking for the truth I've long ignored. You can help me tell this story in a way that will move people. I know that what I've lived through, what I've done, is irreversible. But if I have a chance to change something, I want you to help me do it."

Anna was silent, looking at Carl with an unreadable expression. In her gaze, one could see a battle with her own thoughts. After a moment, she turned her gaze toward the window, where the sunlight lay in a golden streak across the rooftops. She knew that the film she would work on could have a profound impact. She also knew that every decision she made would be scrutinized by the media and the industry.

"If we do this," she began, turning her gaze back to Carl, "there can be no half-measures. I can't afford to work with someone who isn't ready for full commitment. Do you understand?"

Carl nodded, and a shadow of hope appeared in his eyes. He knew this was a chance, but also a challenge that required more from him than he had ever expected.

Work on the film moved forward, and their collaboration was full of tension and challenges. Anna was a perfectionist who wouldn't settle for compromises. When they worked on the script, there were frequent clashes. Every detail was analyzed, every line of dialogue had to be true to the reality they intended to depict. Carl, though used to imposing his will, began to understand that he needed to listen—not only to Anna but to the entire team.

One evening, while they were sitting together over the plan for one of the scenes, Anna paused her work and looked at Carl thoughtfully.

"You know," she said quietly, almost as if speaking to herself, "I used to imagine what it would be like to be in your place. To have power, to make decisions, to direct people. Now, looking at you, I wonder if that power always comes with a price."

Carl looked at her with slight surprise. Her words were like a mirror, reflecting the man he had been years ago—a man who pursued success at any cost. Now that it was all behind him, he understood that the price he had paid had been too high.

"Yes, it has a price," he replied after a moment. "And sometimes you don't realize how high it is until it's too late."

Working on the film was becoming for Carl not just a professional challenge but a path toward understanding what true collaboration meant.

Part III
New reality

Chapter 7

Ethics and new rules

The Hollywood Carl had known years ago was changing before his eyes. From a city full of mysterious deals, manipulation, and hidden dramas, a new reality was slowly emerging. These changes were a response to the turbulent years of scandals, protests, and numerous accusations that had forever altered the structure of the industry. Carl, who had been both a witness and a participant in these events, watched as the world he had built—and which had destroyed him—transformed for the better.

The introduction of new ethical standards was a turning point. An industry that had nurtured a culture of power and hidden the truth for decades now had to face the challenges of equality and transparency. Carl observed as film studios adopted new regulations concerning behavior on set, reporting procedures, and creating safe spaces for all employees. These rules were not just empty declarations; they were tools meant to have a real impact on the work environment.

Carl knew that what he was witnessing was not just the result of legislative actions but also the determination of those who had chosen to speak out about abuses and fight for change. He was aware that his past was part of this dark history, but now he felt he had the chance to participate in something much bigger than himself.

During one meeting at the studio, convened to discuss the new regulations, the atmosphere was tense. Producers, directors, and other industry members, who had grown accustomed to the old rules, found it hard to accept the new realities. Carl sat at the end of the long table, listening to the heated discussions.

"These changes are necessary," spoke the voice of a young producer sitting across from Carl. Her name was Maya, and she had become one of the symbols of the new Hollywood. She fought for equality, transparency, and respect, which should be the norm, not a privilege. "If we want Hollywood to become a place where everyone can feel safe, change has to come."

Not everyone agreed with her. Older members of the industry muttered under their breath. Carl saw it all and remembered himself from the past—the man who couldn't tolerate opposition, who fought for power and influence. Now, however, sitting in this room, he felt something different. A sense of responsibility that he had never known before.

"Maya is right," he spoke up for the first time during the meeting. Everyone turned their heads toward him. "These changes are not just necessary. They're inevitable. The stakes are higher than our reputation. The stakes are the future of this industry and whether we'll be able to look in the mirror without shame."

Carl's words, though spoken calmly, echoed throughout the room. They were more than just a comment—they were a declaration that showed his new identity. Seeing him in this role, many felt that perhaps change really was possible.

When the meeting ended, Carl felt relief, but also a strange sense of fulfillment. The conversations after the meeting were lively, but more constructive. People approached him, some with questions, others with polite words. For Carl, who had been a lone wolf for years, this was a new experience—being part of a process that was not just about fighting for influence but about creating a better future for others.

In the following months, Carl became involved in implementing the new rules. He attended training sessions, led seminars for young producers, directors, and actors, sharing his knowledge and thoughts on responsibility. His story, though still controversial, was becoming proof that change was possible. His words held weight because they came from someone who had experienced both power and downfall.

However, this work wasn't easy. Many still saw him only as the old Carl—the man who represented everything that was wrong with the old system. Some boycotted his seminars, refused to collaborate, or openly said that his transformation was just a façade. Carl accepted this with humility, knowing that he couldn't expect everyone's trust. Every day, he reminded himself that he was working not for his own redemption, but for a future that could look different.

New procedures appeared on film sets. Ethical checks that monitored adherence to the rules were rigorous but necessary. The atmosphere on set began to feel more open, and the actors and crew started to feel safer. For the first time in years, Carl had the feeling that his work served something greater than just achieving success and gaining prestige.

During one of the shooting days, Carl noticed Anna laughing and talking with the rest of the crew. Her relaxed demeanor and joy were a sign to him that the changes really did make sense. She approached him, and her face beamed with a smile.

"You know," she said, looking at Carl, "I used to think this industry would never change. But now, I hope I was wrong."

Carl looked at her and felt, for the first time in a long time, that words were no longer necessary. He smiled gently, knowing that the journey he had taken had been worthwhile.

Chapter 8

Personal reflections

The first words Carl wrote in his journal were uncertain and trembling. "I don't know why I'm doing this," he began, feeling the pen shake in his hand. He stared at the blank pages before him, white like his own thoughts when faced with silence. After years of living in a world where every move had a purpose, every conversation was a strategy, and every glance was a challenge, writing his thoughts on paper felt like an act of strange honesty. It was something he had avoided his entire life, fearing that the truth about himself might be too difficult to accept.

Journaling had started by accident, as a recommendation from his therapist, who suggested it might help him face his thoughts in a more tangible way. At first, Carl had doubts, but one evening, after a day full of meetings and discussions about ethics in the industry, he felt a weight he needed to shed. He sat at the desk in his own home, which had long served only as decoration, and reached for the notebook.

The first entries were chaotic, full of interrupted thoughts and unfinished sentences. "I feel like a stranger in my own life," he wrote one day, only to cross out the words in frustration. Each reflection was an attempt to understand why he had acted the way he did over the years, and what the consequences had been. He began to recall moments that once seemed insignificant—ordinary meetings, innocent words, glances full of unspoken questions. Now, he saw them differently.

With each passing page, Carl became more honest, and his reflections grew deeper. He wrote about power, a taste he knew better than anything else, about how it fueled him, how it fed his ego and sense of invincibility. Power, which had been his obsession for years, now appeared to him as poison—subtle but destructive from the inside. "What is power without responsibility?" he wrote in one of his notes. "Is power without empathy anything other than a tool of destruction?"

He began to consider what his life might have been like if he had never abused his position. These visions were painful because they forced him to face lost opportunities and people he had hurt. He imagined an alternate version of himself—a man who had built his career on respect and collaboration, not fear and domination. These were the visions that came to him at night when sleep wouldn't come, and the only sounds were the ticking of the clock and his own uncertain breath.

In one of the entries, Carl wrote: "If I had the chance to start over, how would I do it? Could I look young actresses in the eye and not see them merely as tools? Could I choose words that build, not destroy?" These questions remained unanswered, but simply asking them was a step forward for him.

The journal became a place where Carl could truly be himself. With each entry, he began to see how much he had lost over the years of his career. He thought about friendships that could have developed if only he had allowed himself a moment of weakness, a human instinct he had always considered unnecessary. He wondered what his relationships might have been like if, at some point, instead of issuing orders, he had listened to those who had the courage to speak.

The hardest reflections were about loss. Not just the loss of power or position, but the loss of his own soul, his own morality. Carl wrote: "Sometimes I feel like I don't know who I am. Am I the man who sincerely regrets, or someone who is just trying to find a way to live in this new reality?" These questions haunted him like ghosts from the past, but they allowed him to understand that the process of change is long and full of difficult moments.

Over time, the notes began to take on a different tone. Alongside reflections on loss, thoughts on responsibility began to emerge. Carl started to realize that his work on the new film, his commitment to industry changes, and the relationships he had begun to build all had meaning. He understood that it wasn't about erasing the past, but learning to draw lessons from it. He wrote: "Responsibility is more than just acknowledging one's mistakes. It's the willingness to act, to change reality, even if the cost is high."

Each new page of the journal was like uncovering another layer of himself—a layer that had once been hidden beneath the façade of certainty and cold calculation. Now, with the perspective of time and experience, Carl began to see that his life could have been different. If only he had stopped for a moment, listened to others, and understood that true strength doesn't lie in domination, but in understanding and compassion.

The journal became not only a place of reflection for Carl but also a bridge to the future. He hoped that one day these entries would help others understand how important it is to recognize the moment when a course can be changed. And if his story could teach someone that change is possible, even after a fall, then he knew his journey had not been in vain.

Chapter 9

Personal reflections

The sun was slowly sinking toward the horizon, painting the sky with warm shades of orange and pink. Carl sat at a small table in a modest conference room, staring at the blank sheet of paper in front of him. The tension in the air was palpable, impossible to ignore. This was the day he had feared for months — a meeting with one of the victims of his past actions. For many years, Carl had tried to suppress the feelings of shame and guilt, pushing away thoughts of those he had hurt, but now, as he waited for her to enter, he felt the past return with double the force.

The door opened slowly, and a woman with short dark hair and a watchful gaze stepped inside. Her name was Eliza, and though her face appeared calm at first glance, it revealed clear signs of fatigue. Her eyes met his, and Carl felt his heart race with fear and uncertainty. There was no distance between them now, no space behind which he could hide. There was only silence hanging in the air.

Eliza sat down across from him, not breaking eye contact. The silence lingered for a moment longer, as each of them gathered their thoughts, trying to understand what they were really doing there. This meeting had been arranged at her request, which surprised Carl. He had expected her to avoid such a confrontation, but her presence spoke of courage and determination—qualities Carl had never been able to find in himself.

"Why did you agree?" Eliza finally asked, her voice soft but carrying a steel core.

Carl took a deep breath, searching for the right words. Dozens of thoughts rushed through his mind, but he knew he couldn't afford empty platitudes. This wasn't an interview; it wasn't a conversation he could steer according to his script.

"Because I owe you this," he answered, looking her in the eye. "I owe you honesty, although I know that no conversation will change what has happened."

Eliza raised an eyebrow, as if these words were both a surprise and a challenge. For a moment, he saw a shadow of pain in her gaze—a pain he recognized, a pain he himself had caused, and now reflected back at him in her eyes.

"Words," she said quietly, "are easy. I've listened to words for years, words that meant nothing. What makes you think they should matter to me now?"

The question struck him harder than he had expected. Carl swallowed and felt a lump rise in his throat. For most of his life, he had believed he could control any situation, that every meeting, every confrontation was a game he knew how to win. Now, looking at the woman whose life he had marked with arrogance and a sense of power, he felt the game losing its meaning.

"I don't have an answer that would satisfy you," he said after a pause, and for the first time, his voice carried a tone he had never used before: honest, devoid of confidence. "I can only tell you that I regret it. I regret it every day. And that I'm trying to understand who I was and who I am now."

Eliza lowered her gaze, and her fingers nervously toyed with the edge of her blouse. The silence that followed wasn't as heavy as before. It had become a transitional stage. They were trying to find a place where they could meet without anger or lies.

"You know, for a long time I thought hate would heal me," she began after a moment, her voice calmer, more reflective. "But it only ate me alive. It took away the strength I needed to move forward. Now, sitting here, I see that hate is something that will never fix the past."

Carl held his breath, feeling her words pierce through him. He understood that this meeting wasn't just for her — it was for him too. It was an attempt to understand whether real change was possible and what forgiveness really meant.

"Can I ask you," he began uncertainly, "what forgiveness means to you?"

Eliza looked up, and in her eyes, Carl saw a mixture of sadness and determination.

"Forgiveness..." she sighed. "It's not something you can just give or take. It's a process that requires time, pain, and understanding. It doesn't mean forgetting or accepting what happened. It's a choice not to let the past define the rest of your life. But I'm not sure if I'm ready to forgive you. I don't know if I ever will."

Carl nodded, accepting her words. They were like a blade, driving deep into his chest.

"I don't expect forgiveness," he said quietly. "I just want you to know that I'm trying to be a better person. That's all I can give you now."

Eliza looked at him with a mix of surprise and relief. In that moment, though forgiveness still felt distant, there was a thread between them that could be the beginning of something new—not redemption, perhaps, but maybe a path toward understanding and peace.

Part IV
Transformation

Chapter 10

Premiere

The evening of the premiere was different from all the ones Carl remembered from the past. Instead of the triumphant marches down the red carpet with a smile full of confidence, he now stood on the sidelines, watching as a spectacle of tension and emotion unfolded around him. The completed film, on which he had worked for the past few months, was more than just a project to him. It was proof of his transformation and an attempt at restitution, a way to show the world that change is possible.

That night, the city was alive with the glow of lights and the flash of cameras. Dozens of journalists, photographers, and film critics gathered in front of the theater that had hosted Hollywood's most important premieres for years. For many of them, the premiere of this film was more than just an artistic event — it was a symbol of the changes that had swept through the industry after the scandals in which Carl had played the lead role.

Standing in the shadows, Carl watched the crowd. The sight of film stars, directors, and producers who had once looked at him with disdain or pity was a mix of uncertainty and curiosity. He watched as Anna, the lead actress and face of the film, stood before the cameras, answering the journalists' questions. Her elegant dress and confident voice added to her charisma, and every movement was a testament to her unwavering determination. He knew that without her, this film would never have been made.

"This is a story about strength, loss, and redemption," Anna said into the microphone, her eyes shining with emotion. "I wanted the audience to see that change is possible, but it requires courage, honesty, and time."

Carl heard those words and felt his heart race. He knew their meaning — they echoed their long conversations, the hours spent on set, and the days when doubts mingled with hope. He was proud of what they had accomplished, but also afraid. He knew that tonight, his past and future would collide in one moment.

When the theater filled to capacity, Carl took a seat at the back. He didn't want to be the center of attention; he didn't want the spotlights to remind him of his past glory. Instead, he wanted to feel how the film affected the audience. The air was thick with excitement and anticipation, and the murmur of conversation quieted when the lights dimmed and the screen flickered to life with the first frames.

The film they had made wasn't an easy spectacle. It was raw, real, filled with emotions that were hard to bear. Carl felt each scene shake him, reminding him of the mistakes and decisions that had brought him here. Seeing the story told through the eyes of the victims, he realized that this story was not only an act of redemption for him but also an attempt to show the world the price of abusing power.

During one of the most moving scenes, when the main character, played by Anna, confesses her story before a crowd, the theater fell silent. The silence was absolute, and the emotions were almost tangible. Carl felt tears welling up behind his eyelids. What he saw on screen wasn't just a story; it was the truth, a truth he had helped write, though he had never been able to admit it before.

When the film ended, the theater paused for a moment in silence. For a few seconds, it seemed as though time had stopped, and then applause erupted. Carl felt the tension leave his body, though his hands trembled slightly. It was the moment he had been waiting for — not a triumph in the style of his former successes, but something much deeper — the recognition that what they had created mattered. Amid the applause, he heard isolated shouts of praise, as well as the sobs of those who felt the power of the story.

After the premiere, Anna approached Carl as people began to leave the theater. Her eyes were filled with tears, but she wore a smile on her lips. For a moment, they stood in silence, looking at each other, and then without a word, she hugged him. It was a gesture full of gratitude and understanding, saying more than a thousand words.

"You've done something great, Carl," she said, pulling back enough to look him in the eyes. "And I know it wasn't easy."

Carl nodded, feeling the weight he had carried for years begin to lift. There was something cleansing about this moment, as if for the first time in a long while, he could breathe freely.

After the premiere, the reviews were mixed, but many critics praised the courage and honesty of the film. It was noted that the story they had told was not only a reminder of the darker sides of the industry but also a call for change. The film became a symbol of new times, and Carl, to his surprise, was recognized as a man who, though burdened with many sins, had dared to face his demons and help others understand that change is possible.

The evening ended with a banquet, but instead of joining in the celebration, Carl chose to take a walk through the city. The streets were alive with activity, and the neon lights illuminated his path. Each step he took reminded him of the past, but now he saw it differently. The past was part of his journey, but it no longer had to define him. Looking up at the stars twinkling in the sky, he felt that he had finally understood what true transformation meant.

Chapter 11

New life

The day after the premiere, as the sun rose over Los Angeles, Carl felt for the first time in years that something had changed within him. It wasn't the euphoria or triumph he had known during the days when his films won awards and broke box office records. It was something more subtle — a sense of peace that soothed his restless heart. He understood that while the past remained indelible, he now had the chance to give meaning to what lay ahead. He decided to start a new life, one not based on domination, but on giving something of himself to others.

Carl began his transformation by seeking out projects that could support the victims of sexual violence. He wanted his work, his experience, and his new approach to contribute to changing the world he had spent years destroying. He reached out to foundations and organizations that worked for women's and children's rights. At first, he was met with distance. For many of those who knew his past, he was a symbol of everything they fought against. Carl knew that trust wouldn't come immediately. This was his new reality — a reality where he had to rebuild from the ground up.

During his first meeting with representatives of one of the organizations supporting victims of sexual violence, Carl felt his heart beat faster. The conference room was modest, filled with photos and posters that reminded everyone of the daily work they did. The representative of the organization, a woman named Lena, looked at Carl sternly. Her eyes were sharp, but her expression was calm.

"Mr..." she began, then hesitated. "Carl. We all know who you are and what happened. Why do you want to help us?"

Carl took a deep breath, feeling the weight of her words. In the past few months, he had learned that he could not avoid responsibility or run from his past. He looked at Lena and the faces of everyone present. He knew that his answer had to be honest.

"I can't undo what I've done," he began slowly, trying to keep his voice steady. "But I can try to help fix the world I helped destroy. I want to support your work. I want to use my resources, my contacts, and my experience to help those who need a voice. I'm not asking for forgiveness or for anyone to forget. I want to act, because I believe change is possible."

Carl's words hung in the air, and the room was filled with painful silence. Lena studied him for a long moment, as though trying to gauge whether his words were sincere. Finally, she nodded, and a faint smile appeared on her face.

"We'll see, Carl. We'll see what comes of this," she said, her voice carrying a note of cautious hope.

The first months of collaboration were difficult. Carl became involved in social campaigns, participated in meetings with victims of violence who wanted to share their stories. Each such meeting was a test for him, reminding him how long the road still was. But he felt that with each passing step, his presence was beginning to take on new meaning. He was not only a symbol of the industry's transformation, but also proof that even the darkest past didn't have to define the future.

One of the most important projects he became involved in was an educational campaign aimed at young people. Carl understood that to change the future, he had to start with education — showing how to build relationships based on respect and equality. He met with students at film schools, talking about his own journey, the mistakes he had made, and how the industry could change. He listened to their questions, sometimes filled with skepticism, but more and more often tinged with curiosity.

One day after such a meeting, a young man named Jack approached him. From the beginning of the meeting, Jack had seemed fascinated by Carl's stories. Jack had a passion that reminded Carl of himself many years ago, but with one important difference — there was no trace of arrogance in his eyes.

"Do you really believe people can change?" Jack asked, his voice full of uncertainty.

Carl smiled slightly, thinking over his answer. "Yes, Jack. I believe everyone can change, but it's not easy. It takes more than I could have ever imagined. It's not just a decision — it's a lifelong process."

As time passed, Carl's relationships with the people he worked with grew increasingly sincere. He learned to listen, not just to speak. His old way of life, based on domination and manipulation, gave way to the need for collaboration and building. In moments when memories returned, when he felt the shadow of shame and guilt, he reminded himself that his task wasn't to erase the past, but to fix what could still be fixed.

At one of the conferences on sexual violence in the film industry, Carl was asked to give a speech. It was another challenge for him, but also an opportunity to talk about the journey he had gone through. Standing before a crowd that looked at him with various emotions — from curiosity to skepticism — Carl took a deep breath.

"I used to believe that power was the only thing that mattered," he began, his voice echoing in the room. "That it justified every action, every decision. But now I know that true strength lies in something else — in the ability to admit mistakes, in the willingness to repair what's been destroyed, and in building something better than what was there before."

The room fell silent, listening to his words. Carl knew he wouldn't convince everyone, but he felt that for some, his story could serve as proof that change is possible. In the crowd, he spotted Lena, who gave him a slight smile, as though saying, "You're starting to understand."

Carl knew that his new life wouldn't be without difficulties, that the past would always be a shadow that sometimes caught up with him. But now, standing on stage, looking at the people with whom he wanted to build a better future, he felt that what he was doing made sense.

Chapter 12

Final reflection

The morning light streamed through the window, bathing the room in a warm, golden glow. Carl stood in front of the mirror in his modest office. It was the same office that once pulsed with life, filled with the sound of phones ringing, conversations about successes, and projects that were supposed to bring him even more glory. Today, however, this space was an oasis of calm, a place where he could breathe and see himself from a new perspective.

He looked at his face, now older, with deep wrinkles that told the story of years full of ups and downs, pain, and transformation. His gaze was no longer cold or full of confidence, as it had been in the past. It was calm, thoughtful, as though he had finally understood something that had eluded him for years.

He paused, remembering how much his life had changed. Once, he believed that power was an end in itself. It had been an obsession, one he had devoted himself to completely. Every move and every word were calculated to benefit him, regardless of the cost to others. That was the Carl he had known for decades, a man living in constant fear of losing his place at the top.

For many years, he hadn't realized how much he had been losing in pursuit of that illusory sense of power. The people he passed by became nothing more than a backdrop, tools for achieving his goals. Even in moments of triumph, there had been an emptiness that he never knew how to name. Now, he understood that this emptiness was the lack of something that now seemed the most important — authentic closeness with others.

He closed his eyes and recalled the moments that had changed his life. The first time he heard the testimony of one of his victims, Anna's gaze during their work on the film, which spoke more than a thousand words, the moments in the therapy center when he had to look deep inside himself, with nothing to distract him. These images were like a mosaic, building a new version of Carl — a man who had learned that redemption wasn't a one-time act, but a long, arduous journey full of doubts and pain.

He looked back into the mirror and saw a man who, though broken by his decisions, had found a way to begin repairing what he had destroyed. It was no longer about successes or climbing the social ladder. Now, it was about giving his best without expecting a reward. This was new to him and surprisingly soothing.

The journal on his desk caught his eye. Over the past years, it had become his companion, a place where he wrote down thoughts he never would have dared to speak aloud. He opened it to a random page and read the words he had written a few months earlier: "There is no courage without fear, there is no redemption without understanding one's own guilt." He reflected on this and felt his heart slow, its rhythm steady with acceptance.

He knew that the path he had traveled was full of pain, but also full of discoveries that had reshaped him. The memories of those he had wronged never left him. Every glance, every story he had heard from the victims, was a reminder of the immense harm he had caused. But instead of being a burden, they became motivation for action. It wasn't about erasing the past, but making sure the future looked different — that it was a place where others didn't have to go through what he had caused.

Carl closed the journal and looked at the wall, where a board hung with the projects he was working on. Each one was about supporting victims, creating safe work environments, and promoting education in the film industry. These were projects that gave him a sense of purpose, connecting his past with the present in a way that allowed him not only to repair but also to create something valuable.

He felt ready to accept the new version of himself — a man changed not by triumphs, but by loss, reflection, and painful redemption. He had become aware of what true responsibility meant, not just toward others but, most importantly, toward himself. He looked in the mirror and saw someone who was able to face his own mistakes and still move forward, building something better, piece by piece.

After years of living under the influence of testosterone, which had shaped his behaviors, thoughts, and needs, Carl discovered how much this inner drive had dominated his life. Sexuality had been like a mask he always wore. His body, desire, heightened senses — all of that, which had once seemed most important, now lost its luster. Finally, after years of unconscious attachment to this need, he understood that his perception of others had been distorted by the filter of desire.

It was only without testosterone, without this pursuit of physicality, that he began to see others as they truly were. Without expectations tied to physical attractiveness or sexual attraction, Carl saw something he had never noticed before: the true faces of those around him. It was like removing the veil from an image he had once seen only in a distorted, sensual light. Now, gaining new understanding, he looked at others in a deeper, more authentic way. Without desire, there was no need to create an idealized image. Instead, he saw people in the fullness of their human nature — with all their complexity, emotions, sensitivity, passions, and fears.

Carl remembered the moment when he realized that life without desire was not only possible but also liberating. Instead of being driven by physical urges, he began to seek a true, deep connection with others. Suddenly, conversations became deeper, more personal, no longer limited to the topics of the body, attractiveness, or sexual expectations. Carl could finally talk about emotions, dreams, fears, and joys — without needing to integrate sexual energy into them.

But that wasn't all. Over time, Carl began to notice changes in himself. He understood that the lack of desire didn't mean giving up on love. On the contrary, life without the pressing urge allowed him to feel love in a purer, more unexpected form. A love that wasn't tied to physical attraction but to a deeper emotional, intellectual, and spiritual connection. A love that was based on true acceptance of the other person, regardless of how they looked, what their history was, or what expectations were placed upon them.

Ultimately, life without desire became for Carl a journey of self-discovery and deeper understanding of himself and others. Instead of chasing fleeting satisfaction, he could see what really mattered. His life had taken on a new dimension, one where there was no place for superficiality and illusion, and the space was filled with the true, priceless value of being together. And while many might see this as losing something important, Carl knew that he had gained something invaluable — freedom. Freedom from the desire that had once shaped his life, and freedom in seeing another person for who they truly were in their purest form.

"This is just the beginning," he said quietly to his reflection, and those words echoed in his heart.

Outside, the city buzzed with life. It was the same as it had always been, yet somehow different, as if his own transformation was part of a broader, ever-changing story. Carl smiled slightly, ready for what was to come.

ISBN 978-83-972526-7-7